The Boy Who Spoke Colors

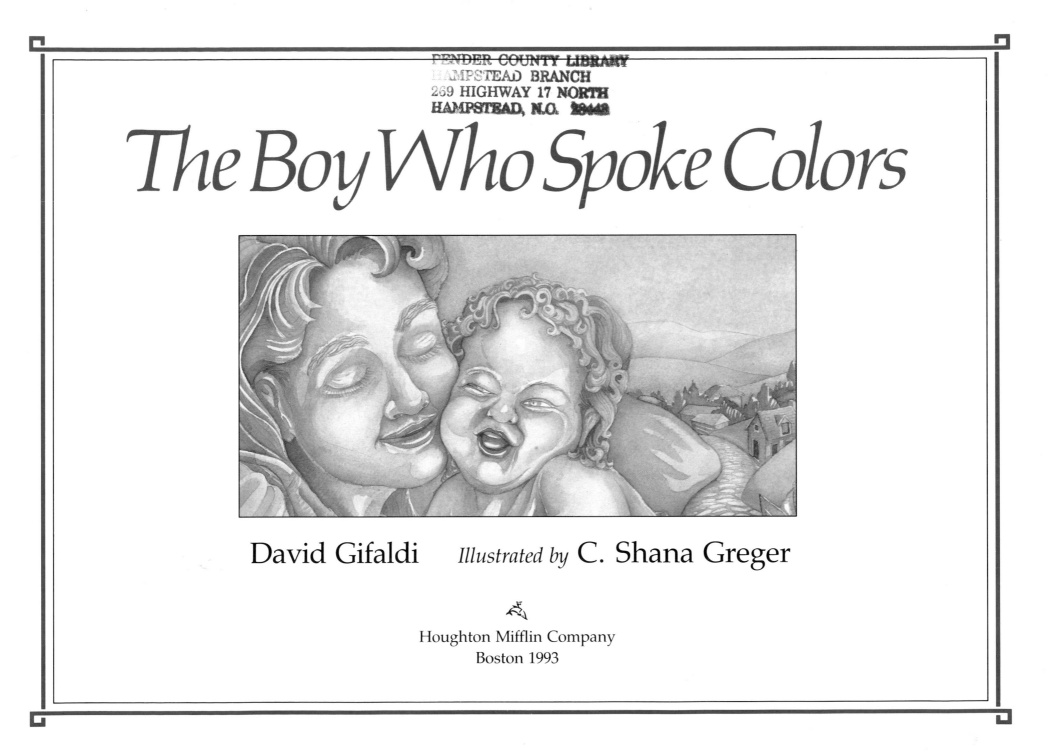

David Gifaldi   Illustrated by C. Shana Greger

Houghton Mifflin Company
Boston 1993

Library of Congress Cataloging-in-Publication Data

Gifaldi, David.
  The boy who spoke colors / David Gifaldi ; illustrated by C. Shana
Greger.
     p. cm.
  Summary: When a greedy king kidnaps Felix, a boy who can
speak only in colors, and tries to exploit that gift, the king
encompasses his own doom.
  ISBN 0-395-65025-9
  [1. Color — Fiction. 2. Greed — Fiction. 3. Kings, queens, rulers,
etc. — Fiction.]   I. Greger, C. Shana, ill. II. Title.
PZ7.G3625Bo   1993   92-11301
[E] — dc20   CIP
                       AC

Printed in Singapore
TWP 10 9 8 7 6 5 4 3 2 1

For Adam, Joshua, Paul, and Brian — D.G.

For Jennifer — C.S.G.

nce, in the faraway north country, there lived a poor peasant named Pavel and his wife, Jobina. The two occupied a tiny hovel on the edge of a village that skirted a deep forest. For years they wished for a child to love, and had all but given up hope when finally a son was born to them. They called him Felix, which means happiness, because that is what he brought them.

Soon Felix was accompanying his parents to the fields, wearing the many-colored scarf Jobina had lovingly pieced together from her best scraps. The scarf served to protect the boy against the wind and made him easier to see as he toddled between the rows.

"But how is it that our child has not yet spoken?" Pavel asked his wife when Felix reached his second birthday.

"Some children speak later than others," Jobina replied. "He will speak soon enough." And the man's concern left him.

After some time, however, Pavel returned home from the village to find Jobina in tears. "Oh, Pavel! Our son has finally spoken. But it wasn't a word at all. He opened his mouth to speak, and out came a puff of color instead."

"Nonsense," said Pavel. "People don't speak colors. Perhaps you nodded off and dreamed such a thing."

Just then the smiling boy climbed upon his father's lap. He pressed his lips together and, with great effort, forced from his mouth a most beautiful shade of blue.

It was then that a beggar happened by and saw a curious glow seeping from the windows and cracks of the hut up ahead. One peek inside, and the man rushed to the village to tell what he had seen. Soon folks were banging on the door of the hut to catch a glimpse of the child who spoke colors.

"Sure, it's the devil's work," shouted one.

"Let us see the boy," said another. "Is he cursed?"

"Go away!" yelled Pavel.

"Leave us in peace," begged Jobina.

But no peace was to be had, for the news had spread even to the king of the realm. Thinking that a boy who spoke colors could be put to good use, the king decided to see the child for himself. He arrived without warning one afternoon while Felix lay napping.

"Your Majesty," said Pavel. "You honor me by stopping here to rest on your journey. I have only water to offer, but please fill your casks."

"My journey ends here," the king answered. "Are you so impolite as to not ask me inside?"

"Surely my house is unfit for a king," Pavel said.

The king scowled, and one of his men kicked open the door. "Where is the child who speaks colors?" the king demanded.

"You must be mistaken, sire," Jobina said with a tremble. "There is no such child here. There is only our boy, Felix, who is mute."

"Let me see this mute!"

Pavel nodded, and Jobina reluctantly gave over the sleeping child. Sensing that he was in the arms of a stranger, Felix awoke with a start and began to cry.

"Now, now," the king said. "I hate bawling children. I order you to cease this demonstration at once."

Although Felix did not understand the king's order, he *did* stop crying. His eyes opened wide at the sight of the king's jeweled sword and splendid robes. He expressed his wonder in a chorus of color more beautiful than any he had spoken before. Even Pavel and Jobina could emit only little cries of *ooh* and *ahh* at what they saw. When the last mists of color had faded, the king came out of his shock to inform the unhappy couple that he would buy their child.

"No!" cried Jobina. "He is ours!"

"We want none of your money," said Pavel. "If you take him, know that you have stolen him and have caused us great misery."

"Indeed. You're lucky I don't have you put to death for such insolence," snapped the king. "Come, let us begin our journey. Leave behind a few coins for these two, though they hardly deserve it."

Jobina ran crazed after the king's coach, waving Felix's scarf as though she had forgotten to dress him warmly enough. Pavel caught up to her and tried in vain to comfort her. The two watched, tears tumbling from their eyes, until the coach was no more than a dot on the horizon.

At the castle, the king ordered a servant girl to look after Felix until he decided how best to make use of the boy's gift. When Katya saw the boy, her heart went out to him, and in time Felix came to trust the girl and to love her gentle ways. He liked it best when Katya sang for him, for her songs were the songs of home. Grateful, Felix sang too, in the only way he could.

One day the king sent for Felix. "Come, my little wonder. It is time for you to begin payment for your stay here." He rushed the boy down steep, echoing stairways and into a windowless room.

"You're to begin at once," said the king. "Just speak a color into a bottle, cork it up tight, and affix my seal. Then shelve the bottle according to color. And be neat about it!" He grinned. "People will pay handsomely for such marvels."

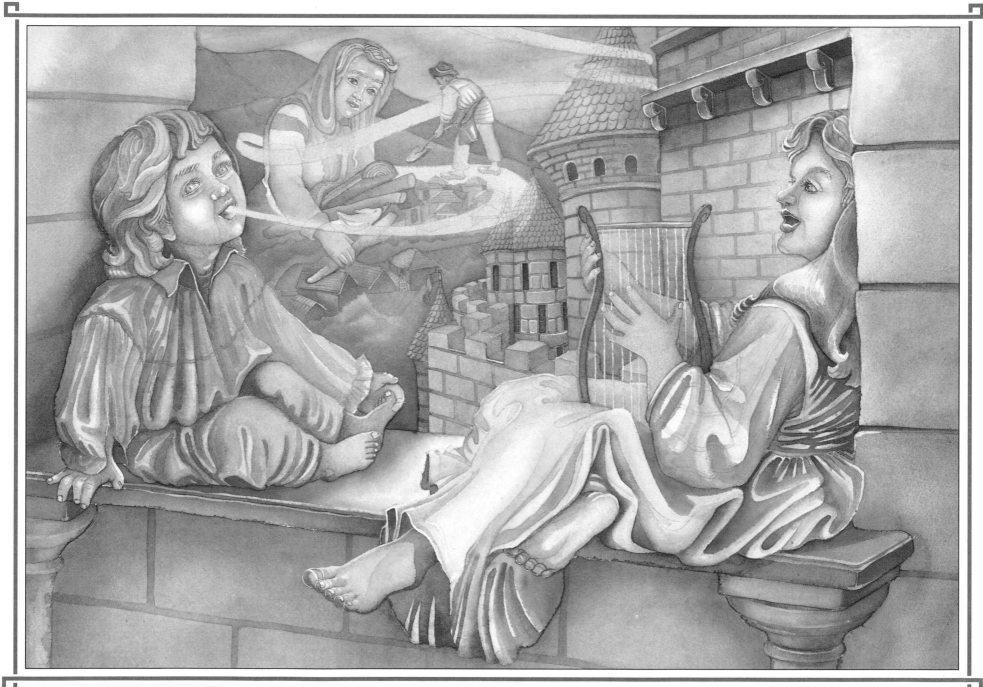

Felix seated himself on the cold stones of the floor. He shook his head, his lips tightly closed.

"You dare defy my command?" said the king. "Bring the girl servant to me at once."

"Now then," he told Felix, when Katya was brought in. "Either you begin working, or you shall never see the girl again."

Tears welled up in Felix's eyes. But still he shook his head.

"Very well," raged the king. "Take the girl and give her to the most hateful man or woman that can be found. So shall she live out the rest of her wretched life."

Felix jumped to his feet. He wanted to shout *NO*, but instead a puff of the clearest, deepest purple soared from his mouth.

"So you have regained your senses," said the king. "Then the girl can stay. For now."

With that the king swung out of the room. Alone, Felix sadly began the task of speaking and bottling his magnificent colors.

Years passed and the kingdom grew wealthy. Everyone wanted to buy the king's colors. An opened bottle or two was the perfect antidote to a cloudy day. Weddings and birthdays were that much more festive with a case of the king's colors. Bottles of black became standard fare at funerals. But no matter what the occasion, the colors would always fade within minutes, so that people had to keep buying more and more. In short, it was the perfect business.

Felix worked every day, even holidays. At night, exhausted, he was led back to his cell. It was for this time that he lived. For no matter what the hour, Katya was there to greet him. Together they ate their meager supper. Then Katya sang story-songs that told of upright people accomplishing brave deeds. And as he listened, Felix vowed to escape one day from the king's scheme, and to return to the man and woman whose laughter still chimed in his memory.

As for Pavel and Jobina, they never lost hope. Each year on the day of Felix's birthday, they took the two or three coins they had managed to set aside and traveled to the castle. Each time they were turned away at the gates by the guards, who laughed at the ragged pair and their thin purse.

So it went: the parents torn from the boy, the boy cut off from his parents, while the king grew fatter and fatter.

Then, on the night of Felix's ninth birthday, Katya told the boy of an old couple she had seen while on an errand. "So sad were their faces, and the guards beat them from the gates as if they were dogs." From her apron she withdrew a faded scarf whose threads barely held together. "In the scuffle, the poor woman fell and dropped this. I called after her, but the guards drove me back."

Trembling, Felix reached for the many-colored scarf. He raised it to his cheek, breathing in the smells of fields, wood smoke, and the salt of his dear mother's tears.

"Oh, Felix," said Katya. "Your parents."

The next evening, Felix refused to eat. Instead he laid out the tattered scarf and began wrapping the chunks of hard bread that were to be his supper. When Katya questioned him, Felix pointed past the window to the forest, his face set with resolve.

"No!" cried Katya. "You will surely be caught, and your troubles will be even greater."

She turned from the boy's steadfast gaze with a sigh. Finally, she said, "You are right. Any chance to be free is worth the risk. We shall go together, for well or for naught."

That very night, carrying only the scarf filled with bread, the two sneaked away from the castle. Years and years of routine had caused the guards to become careless. They slept soundly, never thinking their young charges might try to escape.

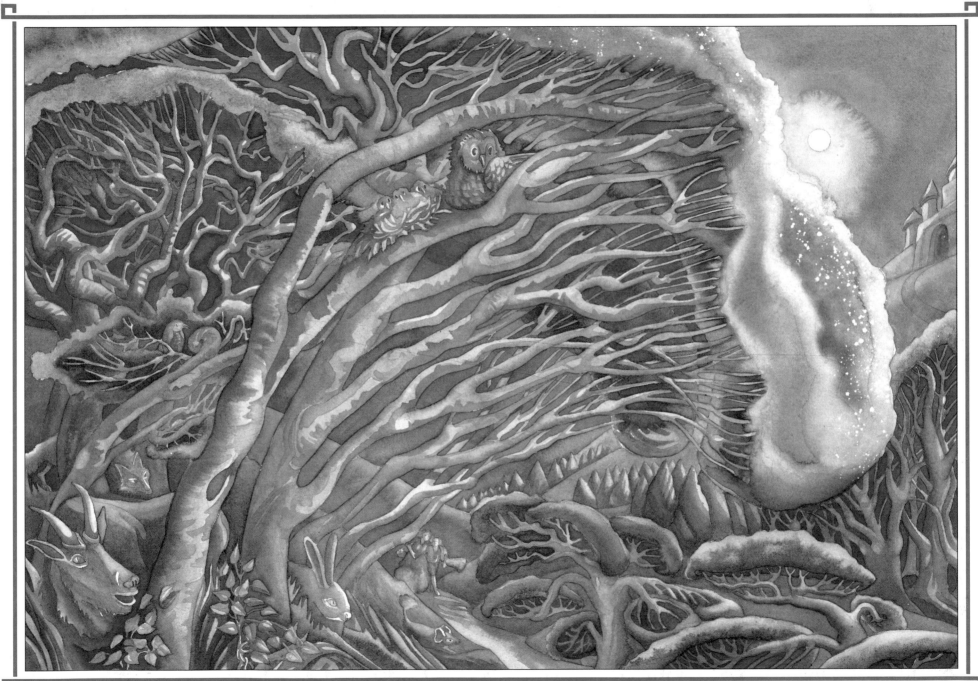

Guided only by starlight, Felix and Katya fled through the great forest. The hungry cries of night animals pricked their ears and turned their blood cold. When dawn arrived, they lay down to rest far from the trail. Upon awakening, they ate, then waited for the shadow of night before continuing. They traveled this way for three nights until they came to the village of Felix's birth.

The boy's eyes shone when he saw the tiny hut set away from the village. He sprang from the forest, beckoning Katya to follow.

"You must take us for fools!" came a harsh voice behind them. The children turned to find the king and his soldiers at the forest's edge. "Seize them!" shouted the king. "And if they should escape again you will all pay with your heads."

Just then a small group approached through the morning mist. In the center were Pavel and Jobina, their hands bound.

"So, you wish to see your parents again?" said the king. "Take a good last look. The two shall swing from an oak this very day."

Pavel couldn't believe his eyes. "Felix!" Jobina cried.

Felix's heart nearly burst with happiness. His mouth opened as if to sing, and out poured a shower of color — colors of joy and sadness . . . of rivers, sunsets, and forest glens. Every color on earth, and some never before seen, passed through his lips. The colors joined like strips of a wondrous garment and took flight, arching higher and higher to the very belly of the sky, then began their descent, spilling back to earth far to the west.

Everyone stood awestruck at the great bridge of color. Felix, no less surprised than the others, felt an unfamiliar stirring in his throat. Trying to rid himself of the strange sensation, he stammered, "*R-r-r*ainbow." Then more forcefully, "Rainbow!"

Had their hands not been bound, Pavel and Jobina would have clapped at their son's first word. As it was, Katya gave Felix a quick hug before a guard wrenched her away.

The king was confused. "And what does all this mean?"

"Your Excellency," said a soldier, "it is said that at the end of such an arc lie more riches than man or woman has ever seen."

"Then we shall follow the arc to its end and take the treasures for our own," the king boasted. "Mount up! Leave the couple behind. The boy and girl come with us."

The group traveled hard over the most rugged country until the horses' mouths foamed white. When at last they came to where the colors met the land, the king and his men gave out shrieks of delight. "Gold!" said the king. "Casks and casks of gold!"

"Rubies!" shouted one man.

"Diamonds!" cried another.

Felix saw no such riches. Only a deep ravine, brilliant with color and light. "They're mad," Katya whispered.

She was right. Through the beauty of Felix's colors, the boulders of the ravine had become a mirage of all that the king and his men had worshiped in life. And rushing to capture what they saw, the men fell headlong into the chasm, their screams of surprise cut off by the telltale snapping of bones on the rocks below.

Felix, Katya, Pavel, and Jobina lived together in peace after that. Having spoken his first word, Felix was quick to learn the language of sound and letters. The villagers called him Rainbow, and the bridge of color that appears after a cloudburst was given the same name.

As for Felix's gift of speaking colors . . . oh yes, it stayed with him. For a gift is forever, and every child born to loving parents is given a gift that can never be erased, no matter how time or evil may conspire against it.

On summer nights, Felix would walk alone among the wildflowers that sloped to the wood, lighting the darkness with waves of blue, silver, and gold. And the villagers would quietly enjoy the wonder, without comment or gossip of any kind.

E

Gifaldi, David

The boy who spoke colors

14.95

E

Gilfaldi, David

The boy who spoke colors